D1249707

FAVOURITE
Animal
STORIES

An illustrated treasury

FAVOURITE Animal STORIES

An illustrated treasury

LITTLE TIGER

LONDON

Contents

Hippety Hoppety
The Cow Who Loved To Dance

Written by Stephanie Stansbie

Illustrated by Barbara Bongini

Hippety Hoppety
The Cow Who Loved To Dance

There was once a cow called Hippety Hoppety who loved to dance. The other cows thought she was a little bit crackers, but that did not bother her one tiny bit. Dancing made Hippety feel on top of the world. She loved nothing more than to shimmy and shake, lunge and leap, jiggle and jive.

"Oh, Hippety," her mother would say, "please stop your twirling and whirling!" But Hippety could not stop.

One day, Hippety was in the middle of the herd, enjoying a little boogie, when she danced right over Grampy Moo's hoof.

"Ooooch!" he wailed. "My poor old toes. Hippety Hoppety – stop!"

"Sorry, Grampy!" Hippety cried, dancing off.

Madame Hoighty Toighty was with her two daughters. "Primula, chew your cud quietly!" she ordered. "Pristina – wipe that mud off your face."

Hippety Hoppety was so caught up in her blissful ballet that she did not notice Madame Hoighty Toighty. She took an almighty leap and landed SPLAT! right in the middle of a muddy puddle. Madame Hoighty Toighty was covered in mud from head to hoof.

"Hippety Hoppety!" she yelled. "How dare you muddy me - you disgraceful, dancing dimwit!"

"I'm so sorry!" Hippety cried, and she ran up the hill out of the way. "Crumbs!" she thought. "That Madame Hoighty Toighty's got a hot temper. She should have a dance once in a while - that'd cool her down." And Hippety set about in a flamboyant flamenco.

Hippety's flamenco was fabulous. It was fiery. It was frenzied! She stamped her hooves and twisted and turned and, as she headed up the hill, Hippety's flamenco got faster and faster and faster, until . . .

CRASH!

Hippety bashed, bottom-first, into a hay bale.
It was such a mighty blow that the huge hay
bale started rolling down the hill.

"Uh-oh!" said Hippety as the first hay bale crashed into the next,
sending them both speeding down the hill where they hit another, and
another and another. Hippety watched in horror as the hay bales headed
towards the herd at a tremendous speed.

"Get out of the way!" she cried, dashing down after them.

At the very last moment, the cows ran helter-skelter, out of the path of the bales. They looked on, shocked, as every single last hay bale rolled into the river at the bottom of the field with a splash!

"Never in all my days . . ." mumbled Grampy Moo.

"I'm s-s-sorry!" Hippety whimpered.

"I told you that cow was trouble!" Madame Hoighty Toighty hissed.

"Hippety Hoppety," said her mother gently, "this dancing is landing you in a lot of trouble."

"But I love it so!" said Hippety.

"Then you must learn to control it," said her mum. "Go and see the sheep for a while. Try and spend the rest of the day just . . . chewing the cud."

"I'll try," said Hippety. And she gave her mum a hug.

Hippety walked slowly down towards the sheep's field. For the first time in a long while, she did not feel like dancing. Her legs were wobbly and her heart felt heavy.

She was just wiping away a tear when she noticed a flurry of fluff down at the bottom of the field. When she saw what was happening, she began to run.

Old Ma Sheep was standing outside the sheep's pen, bleating with all her might. The gate was wide open and all the lambs were pouring out.

"Help me, Hippety!" yelled Old Ma Sheep. "The lambs have escaped from the pen! They're just too fast for me and I'm worried they'll fall in the river!"

"What can I do?" Hippety cried.

"I don't know. But whatever you do, do it quick!"

Hippety had an idea. She started to dance a jig. With a slow stamp of her feet, she circled around the lambs. Then, little by little, her jig became faster. Hippety whizzed round and round the lambs, shepherding them back towards the pen.

What a thud-thud-thud she made with her lightning hooves! Old Ma Sheep could only watch in wonder as Hippety danced and the ground shook.

Just then, one cheeky lamb raced out of the circle and broke free!

"Hippety Hoppety – STOP!" Old Ma Sheep shouted. "Loubie-Lou is heading for the river. I'll never catch her!"

All the other lambs were nearly in the pen. If Hippety stopped her jig now, they would run off again!

"What am I going to do?" she gasped. "A cow can't be in two places at once."

Just at that moment, she saw a wonderful sight. Running down the hill was the entire herd of cows, mooing and cheering as they came. They'd heard the thuds and had come to help.

Madame Hoighty Toighty could not believe what she was seeing. "My word, that Hippety is really some kind of hero!"

"Quick," yelled Hippety. "You have to take over the jig!"

"ME?" Madame Hoighty Toighty cried. "Jig?"

"Ooh yes!" cried Grampy Moo. "Let's dance!"

Hippety chased off after Loubie-Lou, bounding down the hill towards the rushing river. She did a breathtaking somersault and landed in front of Loubie-Lou, just before the little lamb tumbled into the bubbling waters. Loubie-Lou jumped into Hippety's arms, bleating loudly.

"There-there, Loubie-Lou," Hippety sang as she swung and swayed back towards the others.

By now, Madame Hoighty Toighty was leading the herd in a fine, dancing rhythm. And when the last lamb was in the pen, she kicked the gate closed with a stunning scissor twist.

Everybody clapped. Madame Hoighty Toighty and Hippety Hoppety held hands and took a bow.

Hippety's mum wept with pride.

"I feel on top of the world!" Madame Hoighty Toighty whispered to Hippety.

"Dancing will do that for you," Hippety said.

From that day on, Madame Hoighty Toighty danced more and shouted less. And Hippety's dancing never got her in trouble with the herd again . . . well, almost never!

The Great Paper Chase

Written by Josephine Collins

Illustrated by Jo Parry

The Great Paper Chase

On a blustery day down by the river, Squirrel and Mouse were out exploring. Squirrel had spotted something, and was hopping about with excitement.

"There it is! Up there!" he cried. High in the air, a piece of paper was fluttering in the wind. "Quick! Let's catch it!" shouted Squirrel. And he raced off along the riverbank.

"But it's too high. How ever will we reach it?" said Mouse, scampering fast to keep up. Squirrel leapt up to snatch the paper, but the wind blew it just out of his reach.

"Oh my, oh my, bless my whiskers!" gasped Mouse. "We're too close to the edge! We're sure to fall in the river!"

"Ah-ha! Got it!" cried Squirrel, as he sprang up high and pounced. "Just look at this!"

Squirrel proudly held up his find for Mouse to see. "Now this, my young mousey friend, is just what we need for our day of adventuring!"

"But how will we have an adventure?" blinked Mouse, who wasn't so sure he *wanted* a

great adventure. "It's just a piece of paper."

"I'm sure there's all sorts of fun to be had with it!" Squirrel declared.

"Oh my . . . like what?" whispered Mouse.

"I don't exactly know yet," said Squirrel. "But I'm sure Hare will!"

So the two friends set off together to Hare's house. Hare was bustling round his workshop when Squirrel and Mouse burst in.

"Look at this, Hare! What do you think?" cried Squirrel.

"Very interesting," said Hare, examining it with his magnifying glass.

"Of course, it's not the biggest piece of paper I've ever seen," he added.

"But can we have some fun with it?" said Mouse. "Squirrel was sure you'd think of something brilliant!"

"I think we can," grinned Hare, and he laid out the paper on his workbench. Then with a roll and a fold and a tuck . . . "There!" he said.

"You've made a hat! Clever, Hare!" Mouse cried. They all tried it on. It was much too big for Mouse! And it was too small to fit over Hare's huge ears. But it did fit Squirrel perfectly!

"Thank you, Hare. It *is* lovely," said Squirrel, "but I wonder if you might make something a bit more . . . exciting?"

"Let me see," nodded Hare. "Yes! I know just what we can do!" Carefully he folded and tucked the piece of paper, over and over again, until at last he was happy.

"Ta-da!" he cried, holding up a magnificent pointy thing with wings.

"A paper bird! You *are* clever, Hare!" cheered Squirrel and Mouse. And the friends hurried out into the wind to see if it would fly.

"Hold it up high, Mouse!" Hare called. "Then throw, and we can all chase after it, and see where it leads us!"

"OK!" squeaked Mouse. "1 . . . 2 . . . 3 . . . Wheeee-eek!"

A huge gust of wind suddenly blew the paper bird up, up and away – with Mouse still holding on!

"Oh my, oh my, bless my whiskers!" cried Mouse, hanging on tightly to the paper bird as it soared up into the air.

"Mousey! We're coming!" shouted Squirrel.

"Try not to panic!" called Hare, as the two friends chased as fast as they could after Mouse.

Squirrel charged ahead across the field, just managing to keep up. "I might be able to reach him at the top of the bank!" he cried. He raced up the slope, took a leap and flew off the steep edge . . .

"GERONIMO!" he yelled, reaching out. But Mouse and the paper bird were far too high and Squirrel tumbled down with a bump! "The wind's too strong! We're never going to catch him!" he gasped.

"It's all right, I can still see him!" cried Hare. "He's heading towards the river! Come on!"

Squirrel and Hare scrambled down the riverbank just as Mouse and the paper bird were soaring over the water. "He's going to hit the oak tree!" gasped Squirrel.

With a thud and a flurry of leaves, the paper bird nose-dived into the branches at the very top of the tree. "Oh no! Poor Mouse!" cried Squirrel.

"Don't worry! We're going to rescue you!" Hare shouted. They needed to cross the river! The two friends leapt across stepping stones, hopping from rock to rock . . . until there were no rocks left! They both looked at the fast flowing water between them and the tree.

"We're going to have to jump," cried Hare.

With a bounce and a leap, at last, Hare and Squirrel were safely on the other side.

"Phew!" gasped Hare, and they both charged over to the tree.

"Just hold on, Mouse! I'm coming up!" called Squirrel. He scurried up the tree trunk and started leaping from branch to branch. At the very top, he found Mouse swinging upside down, hanging by his tail from the highest branch.

"It's alright, Mousey! I've come to save you!" panted Squirrel.

"Thank you!" said Mouse. "Look, I didn't drop our bird!"

Squirrel lifted Mouse up onto the branch and gave him a piggyback safely down.

"What a relief you're safe, Mouse!" said Hare.

"You must have been very frightened," said Squirrel. "I was so worried."

"Not at all!" said Mouse. "That was the most amazing, exciting ride EVER! Can I have another go, please?"

"Oh Mousey, what a little adventurer you are!" chuckled Squirrel. "But maybe we'd better plan our next adventure for tomorrow! I bet Hare's already got a brilliant idea!"

Little Fox Tells Tales

Written by Becky Davies

Illustrated by Kimberley Scott

Little Fox Tells Tales

It was a sunny day in the forest, and Little Fox was in her garden listening
to her mummy read a story. Little Fox loved stories, and this was one of her
favourites. She sat up on her bench and listened to the tale of monsters and
dragons. But all too soon Mummy Fox closed the book and said . . . "The End."

"Already?" pouted Little Fox.

"Yes, I'm afraid so," laughed Mummy.

"Can we read another – please?"

Just then, Daddy Fox poked his head through the front window. The smell of freshly-baked blackberry pie wafted out after him.

"If you've finished reading I've had a great idea. Let's go and visit Bunny! Blackberry pie is her favourite. We could take her some."

"We're not finished reading, Daddy," protested Little Fox. "We were about to start another book . . ."

"That *is* a great idea!" said Mummy Fox. "Come on, little one," and she went inside to help Daddy pack up the pie. Little Fox stuck out her bottom lip and scowled as she climbed down from her bench. She wanted more stories! Bunny lived all the way on the other side of the forest – it would be hours before they were home again. What could she do?

"Are you sure we can't stay for just one more story?" she called to her parents, hopefully. But they were busy in the kitchen, and didn't hear her.

But Little Fox wasn't about to give up that easily – she looked around, and suddenly she had an idea.

"Wait!" she cried, as Mummy and Daddy walked up the path towards her, a basket in Daddy's paw. "I forgot. A big . . . umm . . . storm is coming today! So we shouldn't go anywhere after all."

"A storm? Are you sure, sweetheart?" asked Mummy Fox in surprise, looking up at the beautiful blue sky.

"Yes," nodded Little Fox. "Maybe we should stay home safely and read stories . . . and eat blackberry pie," she added.

"Oh!" said Daddy Fox, catching Mummy's eye. "Well the storm looks quite far off, Little Fox," he said. "I think we'll be safe enough."

And so the foxes set off into the forest, with Little Fox dragging her
feet at the back. But they had only gone a short way through the trees when
Little Fox called out.

"Wait! I think we should go back. It's too dangerous! There are huge,
enormous, scary grumblegrousers in the woods!" And she pointed to a
footprint on the ground.

"Hm, really? That looks like a fox footprint to me," said Mummy Fox,
as she walked back to Little Fox and held out her hand. "Come on, Little
Fox. We'll protect you from any grumblegrousers we may find, we promise."
And she winked at Daddy Fox.

"The sooner we get to Bunny's, the sooner we'll be home again,"
added Daddy.

Little Fox held onto Mummy's hand for a while, but when they got to the bridge over the river she pulled away.

"Wait!" she cried. "We can't go any further because . . . because . . ." she looked at the water for inspiration, "there are giant . . . snafflesnappers in the river!"

This time Mummy and Daddy looked at each other.

"Well we'll just have to put you out of their reach then, won't we?" said Mummy, lifting Little Fox up onto Daddy's shoulders.

"I know you wanted more stories," said Daddy Fox gently, bobbing Little Fox up and down on his shoulders, "but do you think you were maybe imagining the monsters so we could get home sooner?"

Little Fox stuck out her bottom lip, but then nodded slowly.

"You must try not to tell tales, Little Fox," said Mummy. "Stories belong in books, and yours will still be there when we get back."

"Sorry, Mummy," said Little Fox, "sorry, Daddy."

"OK darling. Maybe you could tell one of your own stories to Bunny with that imagination of yours?" said Mummy.

Little Fox thought about this quietly for a moment, before saying, "OK Mummy. But I'll need extra pie, for energy!" and they all laughed.

The rest of the journey went quickly for the three foxes. Little Fox picked flowers with Mummy, and raced with Daddy, and chatted away until she had quite forgotten that she had wanted to stay at home. They were almost at Bunny's house when Little Fox heard a noise. She pricked up her ears. Maybe there really was a grumblegrouser in the woods after all. There it was again!

"Help!" called the voice.

"Wait!" cried Little Fox to Mummy and Daddy. "I heard a voice coming from over there!" and she pointed to a blackberry bush further back on the path.

"I thought we'd spoken about this," sighed Mummy Fox. "You really must stop telling tales, Little Fox."

"But it's true, it's really true!" Little Fox protested, stamping her foot.

"That's enough, Little Fox," said Daddy, but Little Fox had already dashed back up the path towards the voice.

"HELP!" it cried loudly. It was coming from inside the bush! Little Fox pushed the spiky branches aside, and there she found . . . Bunny!

"Oh Little Fox!" Bunny cried when she saw her, "I'm so pleased to see you! I'm stuck, and I thought no one would ever come to help me!"

"Don't worry, Bunny," said Little Fox, "we'll get you out!"

Mummy and Daddy Fox were already running down the path towards her. They were very surprised to see Bunny in the bush! Together, Mummy and Daddy helped Little Fox gently prise the thorny branches away from Bunny's fur.

Back at Bunny's house, Mummy made them all some honey tea.

"We're sorry for not believing you, Little Fox," said Daddy. "Thank goodness you heard Bunny calling!"

"You were very brave," added Mummy.

Little Fox minded only a very little bit that they hadn't listened to her – after all, she *had* been telling tales first. She minded even less when Mummy presented her with a HUGE slice of the warmed blackberry pie and called her a hero.

"But, Bunny," she said suddenly, "what were you doing in the bush?"

"Picking blackberries of course," answered Bunny, "to bring to my favourite foxes!"

As they all munched their pie, Bunny brought out a surprise for Little Fox. It was a new book for them all to read together! And so, tummies full of pie, the three foxes snuggled into their cushions as Bunny opened the first page. "Once upon a time . . ."

43

The Best Present

Written by Josephine Collins

Illustrated by Ian Cunliffe

 # The Best Present

Cat and Dog lived together but they were definitely not the best of friends. Cat thought Dog was noisy, clumsy and a bit smelly, and Dog thought Cat was grumpy, fussy and very selfish.

One morning, just like every morning, Cat woke early. She stretched her silky paws, and quietly padded downstairs, taking care not to wake Dog. "Perfect," she purred. "Morning milk time just for me!"

But soon she heard a scramble of paws heading her way. "Bother that stinky Dog! He's up already!" she sighed.

"Cat! Cat! Cat! I've seen something!"
yelped Dog, charging into the kitchen
and knocking into Cat's bowl of milk.
"Whoops!" he panted.

"Slow down, clumsy! What do you mean?" asked Cat.

"At the back! On the doormat! Something amazing! Presents!" cried
Dog, running around the kitchen.

Cats eyes lit up. "Presents! That does sound interesting!" And she raced
Dog to the back door.

Cat and Dog took a good look at the presents. There were two of them,
neatly wrapped in lovely paper with pictures of cats and dogs on it.

"Well, they are most definitely for us," said Cat. "And there are two, so that means one each." Cat and Dog stared at each other, wondering who should have which present. Suddenly they both made a grab for one.

"This nice, small one is perfect for me," purred Cat.

"Yippee! This big, squashy one is just right for me!" cheered Dog.

"See you later, Dog!" said Cat.

"Ta-ta, Cat!" said Dog. And they both scampered off to enjoy their presents alone.

Feeling very pleased with herself, Cat sauntered off to her favourite spot by the window. From here, she could see the whole garden, and keep an eye on Dog. "What have we here?" Cat mewed, as she unwrapped a soft, cuddly mouse. "You are just right for a fabulous cat like me!" Then she tossed her new toy up into the air for a game of pounce and catch.

Meanwhile, Dog had trotted out into the garden with his present. He found a nice patch of dirt behind a bush, and then tore open his parcel. "Wowee!" he said, shaking out a woolly patchwork blanket. "This is the best present EVER!" And he dived onto the blanket, stretched himself out and fell fast asleep.

After several rounds of throwing her mouse and chasing it, Cat was a bit fed up. The game wasn't much fun all by herself, so she decided to have a little snooze instead. But then she spied Dog in the garden. "That's not fair! That stinky dog has got a better present than me! I'd have the best snooze EVER on that blanket!" she moaned. She scampered down the stairs and marched into the garden to find Dog.

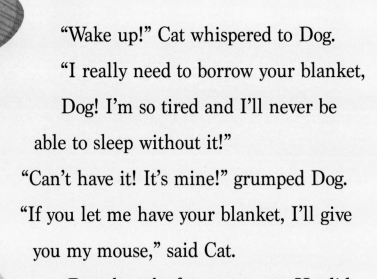

"Wake up!" Cat whispered to Dog. "I really need to borrow your blanket, Dog! I'm so tired and I'll never be able to sleep without it!"

"Can't have it! It's mine!" grumped Dog.

"If you let me have your blanket, I'll give you my mouse," said Cat.

Dog thought for a moment. He did like the look of the mouse. Maybe it was a better present after all . . . So Dog agreed.

Back at her favourite spot, Cat purred with pleasure as she stretched out on the soft, cosy blanket. She didn't even mind its slightly doggy smell. But she just couldn't settle.

"I wonder what that stinky dog is doing with my mouse?" she fretted. Cat looked out of the window and saw Dog having a wonderful time with the mouse. "That's not fair!" she cried. "Why is Dog having so much fun? I want my mouse back!"

Dog had enjoyed a really good chew of the mouse, and was now having fun burying it in some leaves. All of a sudden, Cat appeared.

"Hi Cat!" said Dog.

"Can I have my mouse back, oh pleeease!" cried Cat.

"Only if you give me my blanket back," said Dog.

Cat thought about the soft, snuggly blanket, and the lovely snooze she wanted to have on it. "But I want both presents!" she cried.

"That's not fair! Why are you so selfish?" gasped Dog. But then he had an idea . . . they could share the presents!

Cat and Dog both stared at the mouse.

"So how do we share it then?" Cat sniffed.

"Let's bury it!" suggested Dog.

"No, let's chase it!" argued Cat. So they tried both games. Then they made up some new games. And before long, they were having so much fun playing together that they forgot to be grumpy.

"This is fun!" purred Cat.

"Yep!" said Dog. "You're all right sometimes – for a cat!"

Then he yawned a huge yawn – it was time for a nap! Dog curled up on the blanket, leaving a nice cat-sized space beside him. They both fit on the blanket perfectly. The two friends snuggled up on their blanket, with their mouse, and had one of the best sleeps ever!

Samantha The Pink Hippo

Written by Stephanie Stansbie

Illustrated by Hannah Wood

Samantha The Pink Hippo

Samantha was the brightest, bounciest hippo in the jungle. The other hippos loved having Samantha around. She always had a smile for everyone - like a ray of sunshine on a cloudy day. And there was something else very special about Samantha . . . she was pink!

Samantha loved being pink. It was fun and bright, and it was her favourite colour. But being pink wasn't always easy . . .

One day, the hippos were playing hide-and-seek by the edge of the jungle. "I'll count first!" shouted Duncan, who always had to be first.

Samantha ran and hid behind a bush.

". . . 8, 9, 10. Coming! Ready or not!" called Duncan.

But when he opened his eyes, the first thing he saw was Samantha's pink nose, flashing through the leaves. "That's too easy!" he moaned. "Samantha's too pink – I saw her straight away. I want another go." And he started counting all over again.

"Oops!" giggled Samantha. "Sorry!"

"Quick! Hide with me," whispered Maeve, and they ran off together to hide behind a rock. But there wasn't that much room and Samantha's ears poked out at the top.

"Hah!" shouted Duncan, as soon as he'd finished counting. "I can see you again, Samantha. And, ooh look, I've found Maeve too!"

"Harrumph!" mumbled Maeve. "You can hide on your own this time, Samantha."

So Samantha went sadly to hide on her own. But Duncan spotted Samantha's bright pink bottom, and he started to giggle.

"Pinkie Peek-a-boo! I see you!" he sang, and that made him laugh even more.

Samantha had hidden her head deep in the undergrowth, so she didn't hear Duncan laughing. But when the others saw Samantha's bright pink bottom they all started laughing too and joining in the song:

"Pinkie Peek-a-boo! We see you!"

Samantha came out slowly from behind the bush. When she realised why her friends were laughing, her face turned an even brighter pink. Samantha turned away in tears and ran off into the jungle.

It was hot in the jungle and vines caught against her feet, but Samantha kept going until she didn't have any more puff. Then she sat down on a log and wept.

"Being pink is rubbish," she blubbed. "Oh why can't I be the same colour as everyone else?" Then she plonked herself down in the mud and rolled around to make herself grey.

Suddenly, out of the trees sprang the most magnificent bird. He had a spray of fine feathers and fabulous fans for wings. He was the pinkest pink Samantha had ever seen.

"Wow!" she whispered.

The bird shook out his feathers and started to strut, shaking his tail in the most dramatic way and twittering, "Who's that grumbling? What's wrong with being pink?" Then he threw back his head and started to sing:

"*Don't be down in the dump-dump-dumps.*
No one likes a hippo with the grump-grump-grumps.
I'm plucky and I'm lucky – a-rink-a-dink-dink.
I'm a beautiful bird and I'm pink-pink-PINK!"

"You're amazing!" Samantha cried, jumping up and down and clapping her hands.

"Oh, I know," said the bird. "But what about you?"

"I'm not amazing," said Samantha sadly. "I'm Pinkie Peek-a-boo and I'm terrible at hide-and-seek."

"Fluff and nonsense!" said the bird. "You are what you are and you should be proud to be pink. Now, I'm a busy bird and I can't dilly-dally any longer!" Then he took a deep bow and flew off into the trees, singing loudly all the way.

Samantha sat on the log a little while and had a think. She looked at the insects all around her – some brown, some green, some bright red with spots.

"That bird is right. Being pink IS wonderful," she thought. "How boring it would be if everything was just one colour." Then she stood up tall, brushed the grey mud off her skin and trotted back towards the others.

When she got to the edge of the jungle, she heard her friends chatting. Samantha stopped still. "What if they're still laughing at me?" she thought. But she needn't have worried . . .

"I'm bored!" said Duncan. "I wish Samantha was here."

"Me too," said Maeve. "Life is so GREY without her to play."

"I'm back!" shouted Samantha, crashing out through the leaves. Then she shook her beautiful pink behind and sang.

"Who's that down in the dump-dump-dumps?

No one likes a hippo with the grump-grump-grumps.

I'm plucky and I'm lucky – a-rink-a-dink-dink.

I'm a beautiful hippo and I'm pink-pink-PINK!"

Samantha's friends ran over to give her big hugs, cheering and clapping.

"We're so sorry!" said Maeve. "We won't laugh at you again."

"You can laugh if you like," Samantha cried. "As long as I'm laughing too!" And she shimmied her hips and danced and sang until all her friends joined in too. Then they jiggled and wiggled together in a wonderful hippo-rumpus until the bright pink sun set over the jungle.

Looking For Little Bear

Written by Libby Walden

Illustrated by Lucy Fleming

Looking For Little Bear

Bluebird and Little Bear were the best of friends, and every day they would meet at their special tree stump in the forest. Today they were playing their favourite game – hide-and-seek.

"I'll hide. You seek!" chirped Bluebird happily.

"One, two, three . . ." Little Bear counted carefully on his paws.

Bluebird tried hard not to rustle the leaves as she peeped out from her hiding place. "He'll never find me here!" she thought confidently. But then . . .

"BOO!" shouted Little Bear from behind her.

Bluebird got such a fright that she fell off the branch and landed in a pile of crisp autumn leaves.

"Ok, it's your turn to hide now, Little Bear," giggled Bluebird.

But just then they heard the rumbling voice of Mummy Bear calling - it was time for Little Bear to go home. "Awww just five more minutes!" they called back. "Pleeeease!"

"We have to go *now*, Little Bear. Winter's nearly here and there's so much still to do," insisted Mummy Bear.

"Oh all right!" said Little Bear sadly. "Sorry Bluebird, I've got to go. Oh! Before I forget, there's something I haven't told you, you see . . ."

"Now, Little Bear!" insisted his mother, pulling him gently towards home. "That's OK, you can tell me tomorrow," chirped Bluebird. "See you in the morning!"

The next morning, the wind had turned chilly and frost sparkled in the morning sun. Bluebird flew down to the tree stump to meet Little Bear, but there was no sign of him anywhere. She perched on the edge of the stump, tapping her feet and flapping her wings to keep warm.

"Where could he be?" she wondered. "Perhaps he's already hiding. That would be a good surprise. I'd better go and find him!" So Bluebird set off to look for her friend.

First she headed to the big fallen tree on the edge of the wood. Little Bear always went there first when they played hide-and-seek. She landed silently on top of the tree trunk and listened hard – someone was definitely in there! Smiling to herself, Bluebird puffed up her chest and ruffled her feathers, ready to give Little Bear the fright of his life.

"BOO!" she cried, as loudly as she could.

"Argh!" shrieked a voice, and a fox jumped out of the tree trunk looking rather shocked. "You frightened the life out of me!" he grumbled.

"I'm so sorry, Mr Fox! I'm looking for my friend, Little Bear. I think he's playing hide-and-seek," said Bluebird.

"That sounds like fun," replied Fox. "I'll help you look!"

Fox and Bluebird soon arrived at Little Bear's next favourite hiding place – a mossy boulder by the river. They could hear a snuffling sound coming from the other side. Could it be Little Bear?

Very quietly Fox whispered, "3, 2, 1 . . ."

"BOO!" they both shouted at the tops of their voices.

"Eeeek!" came a squeak that definitely wasn't Little Bear!

"Goodness!" exclaimed a disgruntled looking rabbit, wagging her paw at them. "I nearly hopped right out of my skin!"

"Sorry, Mrs Rabbit!" said Bluebird. "We didn't mean to frighten you. We're looking for Little Bear – he's playing hide-and-seek!"

"What fun!" smiled Rabbit. "Can I play too?"

"Of course!" replied Bluebird. "We've got lots more places to look."

The three new friends played all day. They had a wonderful time, but they didn't find Little Bear anywhere.

"I thought he was playing hide-and-seek, but now I'm not so sure. Maybe something's wrong," said Bluebird.

There was only one place left to look – Little Bear's home. As they approached the cave they could hear a loud rumbling coming from the entrance.

"Can you hear it?" squeaked Bluebird in terror. "Someone's got Little Bear. I think they're hurting him." And she flew ahead as fast as her wings could carry her into the dark cave. Fox and Rabbit raced after her and, as they peered inside, the noise got louder and louder.

BEAR'S HOME

"Zzzzzzzzzzzzzzzz," rumbled Mummy Bear.

"ZZZZZZZZZZZZZZ," grumbled Daddy Bear.

"Zzzzzzzz," snuffled Little Bear.

There in the cave was the whole Bear Family. And they were all fast asleep.

"Of course!" sighed Bluebird in relief, "He wasn't playing hide-and-seek at all. Little Bear is hibernating! That's what he was trying to tell me yesterday!"

Slowly the animals tiptoed back out of the cave into the woods, where the sun was beginning to set.

"Well thank goodness we found him!" laughed Rabbit.

"That was brilliant fun!" giggled Fox.

"Little Bear definitely won that game," agreed Bluebird. "But we've got all winter to find new hiding places!" she added mischievously.

What a wonderful day it had been. Bluebird had only been looking for Little Bear, but she had found two new friends along the way. And when Little Bear awoke in the spring, they would have the best game of hide-and-seek ever!

Oh Deer, Barney!

Written by Becky Davies

Illustrated by Richard Watson

Oh Deer, Barney!

It was a very big day for Barney the deer and his friends Beaver, Bear and Skunk. They were going to play by the river, and as they were getting older their mothers had agreed they could go all by themselves!

"What shall we do when we get there?" asked Beaver excitedly. "I think we should build a dam first! I practised with Daddy last weekend and I'm getting really good now!"

"We'll never get there if you don't hurry up," laughed Bear, running ahead. "Now come on, I want to show you all how great I am at catching fish!"

"Slow down, Bear! You and Barney are so FAST now!" protested Skunk. "And I don't think we should go IN the river at all – it's deep and cold and full of creatures. Brrr! Let's play on the grass in the sun instead!"

"What do you think, Barney?" they all asked.

"I think . . ." said Barney, looking at his friends with a gleam in his eyes, "we should . . . RACE!!" With that, they dashed through the trees towards the river together, shouting and laughing all the way.

"I'm going to catch you!" cried Barney, chasing Bear down the riverbank. But Bear raced ahead and crashed into the shallow waters first. "Winner!" crowed Bear.

The friends joked and splashed in the shallows until at last, breathless, they stopped for a drink. Barney lowered his head to the water to take a gulp . . . and that's when he saw them. Poking out of Barney's head were what looked like two very small trees! He had TREES growing out of his head!

"Argghhhh!" spluttered Barney. "Bear! Help!"

"What is it?" said Bear, rushing over.

"Barney, what's wrong?!" gasped Beaver, racing up.

"Tell us, Barney!" cried Skunk, eyes wide. "Is it a snake? An alligator? I told you so! Get away from the water!"

"I have trees!" Barney shouted. "Trees! Growing out of my head!"

Barney's friends just smiled at him.

"Oh," said Skunk, "is that all?"

"IS THAT ALL?" cried Barney. "Look at me! How did this happen?"

"They've been there for ages now, Barney," said Bear gently.

"We thought you knew," added Beaver.

"No, I didn't!" Barney said, turning his head this way and that and looking at his reflection in the water. He felt panic rising in his tummy.

"Isn't it wonderful!" said Skunk, beaming.

Barney turned to Skunk, confused. How could this be wonderful?

"Trees are really great," insisted Skunk. "Skunks get food from them, like leaves and berries. When yours get bigger we could have a special hoard just for us! That's what you should use your trees for!"

"Oh yes!" cried Beaver. "Trees are really useful, Barney! Beavers couldn't build dams without them, and my daddy said that dams are important for LOTS of things, like helping stop flooding." He puffed himself up importantly, and turned to Skunk and Bear. "When his trees get bigger and grow high into the sky that's what he should use them f—"

"I've got a better idea!" interrupted Bear. "He could use his trees as scratching posts for claw sharpening! Bears would come for miles around to sharpen their claws against his magnificent trees - when they get bigger, that is."

Delighted, the friends turned back to Barney to see if they had cheered him up. But poor Barney just burst into tears and galloped into the trees.

"I want my mum!" he cried. And he didn't stop running until he was all the way home.

"What ever has happened, Barney?" asked Mum worriedly, as Barney crashed up the front path, sobbing. "Have you fallen out with your friends?"

Barney shook his head and then told her, between hiccups, all about the trees. ". . . and then they said that they would grow high into the sky! What will I do, Mum?" Barney wailed.

"There's no need for tears, my little one," said Mum, drying Barney's face. "Come with me – I'll show you." And she led Barney through the trees.

He followed her until they reached a clearing. And there he saw a group of deer . . . all with trees just like his!

"You see they're not trees, Barney my love," said Mum, "they're antlers! They show you're growing up big and strong. Antlers are very special, and you should be proud of them."

Barney looked at the deer in front of him, each with a pair of truly magnificent antlers, and felt his worries fade away.

"Wow!" he whispered.

Just then Bear, Beaver and Skunk came charging through the trees. "Barney!" they called. "We didn't mean to upset you!"

"We ran all the way from the river," said Beaver, "but you're too fast for us!"

"We're sorry if we said something wrong," added Bear.

"You can do whatever you want with your trees, we promise," finished Skunk.

"But look!" said Barney, pointing at the group of deer. "My trees aren't trees at all – they're antlers!"

"Antlers?" Bear repeated. "Then we won't use them as scratching posts?"

"Or for dam building?" asked Beaver.

"Or to gather food?" said Skunk.

"No," replied Barney, gleefully. "Isn't it wonderful!"

The friends looked at Barney's beaming face, and paused for just a moment before . . .

"Hooray!" they all cheered. Barney was thrilled, and everyone made a big fuss of him and his antlers for the rest of the day. Bear, Beaver and Skunk were very happy for their friend, and only a tiny bit disappointed that the trees weren't trees after all.

Patch Saves
The Day

Written by Jenny Hepworth

Illustrated by Jo Parry

Patch Saves The Day

One sunny day on Meadow Farm, five black and white puppies named Buster, Bruiser, Penny, Polly and Patch were playing games in the farmyard. Patch was very small, and though he tried hard to keep up with his bigger brothers and sisters, his little legs meant he couldn't jump very high, or run very fast, and he kept coming last.

"You're just too small to play with us, Patch," scoffed the other puppies. "You'll never be big enough to join our gang."

"Never mind, Patch," said their mother, Sally, trying to cheer him up. "It's not your size that's important. It's your courage and your spirit that really matter."

"Let's play a new game," said Buster, the biggest pup. "It's called Chicken Chase! You have to sneak up on the chickens, then bark as loud as you can to make them jump."

"Why don't you go first, Patch?" offered Bruiser. "Even you can probably play this game!"

"Great!" said Patch happily. "Just watch me – I'll show you how it's done!" Patch crept forward, as quiet as quiet, till he was right next to the hens. Then he took a deep breath, threw back his head and . . . YIP! out came a tiny little yap!

The other puppies rolled around on the ground laughing until their tummies hurt, and the chickens didn't so much as turn a feather! "Call that a bark?" giggled Penny. "I've heard louder noises from a mouse!" And they all laughed some more. Even the chickens cackled quietly to themselves.

"Oh please let me try again. Please!" said Patch. "I was just getting started!"

"Sorry, Patch – you're just too small for our games. Come back when you've grown a bit bigger," said Polly, trying to be kind.

Poor Patch plodded slowly away. "I can't help being little," he murmured sadly. Just then he spotted a beautiful butterfly floating past on the breeze. "I bet I can catch that," he thought, and he bounded after it.

Patch chased the butterfly all through the meadow until he came to a rusty oil barrel that was lying on its side. The sun was shining and the barrel was warm and snug. Feeling tired and sad, the butterfly forgotten, Patch curled up and soon fell asleep.

When Patch awoke he yawned and stretched. "I wonder if my brothers and sisters have missed me," he thought sleepily, peeping out to see what was going on in the farmyard. But to his horror he saw an enormous fox sneaking towards the chickens, who were grazing in the afternoon sunshine. His mother had told him that foxes could be very dangerous.

Patch stayed still – hardly daring to breathe as the fox crouched down, ready to pounce. "Oh no!" he wailed. "I've got to warn them. But I'll never get there in time with my little legs!"

There was only one thing to do. Patch took a deep breath, opened his mouth and . . . out came a deafening WOOF! WOOF! WOOF! as his bark echoed around the barrel. The noise was so loud and the sound so fierce he even scared himself. Peeking out of the barrel, he saw the fox running away in fright.

"Wowee!" shouted Patch. "I did it. I really did it!"

The other animals had heard the noise and soon the whole of the farmyard was in a flap. The chickens were squawking, the cows mooing, the sheep baaing, and the other puppies were barking so loudly that Patch's mother came running over to see what all the fuss was about.

"A naughty fox tried to eat the chickens but a big, brave dog scared it away. Its bark was so loud, it must be HUGE! It came from the old oil barrel!" the puppies told Sally excitedly.

"Thank goodness the fox is gone. Is everyone OK?" said Sally, counting her puppies. "One, two, three, four . . . Where's Patch?" she asked.

The puppies all looked at their paws.

"We haven't seen him for ages," said Penny in a worried little voice.

"We need to find him," said Sally. "I wonder if that big dog can help."

Sally marched over to the barrel to talk to the big dog. But to her surprise, instead she found . . . PATCH!

"Patch! You're OK! Thank goodness," said Sally, licking his ear.

"But where's the big, brave dog gone?" asked Bruiser, rushing up. "The one with the really loud bark?"

"It wasn't a big dog," giggled Patch. "It was me! Watch and I'll show you!" WOOF! WOOF! WOOF! he barked, and the noise echoed round the farmyard. The puppies thought it was wonderful.

Finally, when the noise became too much, their mother said, "Haven't you got something you'd like to say to Patch?"

The pups stopped playing, and Buster spoke for them all. "Patch, you scared away the fox and saved the chickens. We're sorry we said you were too small – you're the bravest of us all."

"That's OK," laughed Patch. "I know now that I'm not too small – I'm just the right size!"

Patch was a hero, and from that day on the other puppies always let him join in their games. Sometimes he even wins!

Otter's Ocean Adventure

Written by Emily Hibbs

Illustrated by Lucy Fleming

Otter's Ocean Adventure

Little Otter dived off the slippery rock, too impatient to sit still any longer. Today his dad was taking him out into the open ocean for the first time ever! The early morning sunlight danced across the water. It was a perfect day for swimming.

"You don't seem nervous at all," said his friend Turtle, sounding impressed.

"Why would I be nervous?" said Little Otter. He knew he was the best swimmer in the ocean, and he couldn't wait to prove it.

"Little Otter! There's a pod of dolphins on the other side of the cliff. Maybe you'll see one!" Puffin said, landing on the rock.

"Dolphins are so much fun!" said Seal. "And not far from here there are colourful rocks called coral—"

"Actually, coral isn't rock," said Daddy Otter, swimming up alongside them and smiling broadly. "It's made up of millions of little animals."

"No way!" Little Otter cried in amazement. "Can we go and see them?"

"We will soon," said Daddy Otter. "But today, we'll just get used to the ocean. Ready? Stay close, Little Otter!"

Calling goodbye to his friends, Little Otter rolled over and paddled with his back legs alongside his dad.

"That's it!" encouraged Daddy Otter. "Propel with your tail as well."

Little Otter put on a burst of speed. He hadn't forgotten about his tail, of course. He was just warming up.

They swam out into the open ocean and soon the beach was a thin line on the horizon. Little Otter listened as Daddy Otter showed him how to feel for strong currents and pointed out good spots to find food.

"It's important to keep an eye on the weather, too. You see those big grey clouds gathering—"

"Look at that bird!" Little Otter interrupted, catching sight of a seagull plummeting into the water and scooping a silver fish from the waves.

"Did you see it?" he asked excitedly. "It went under the water like this!" Little Otter tried to copy the seagull, flipping up his back legs and diving under the waves.

"Wow!" he said. The water was full of life. Hundreds of fish darted this way and that, their scales glittering as they caught the sunlight.

Out of the corner of his eye, he spotted something ambling along the sand on the ocean floor. A gentle paw pulled him back to the surface.

"What's that creature called?" Little Otter
asked, spluttering a little as he caught
his breath. "It had a big shell, like
a crab, only longer."

Daddy Otter laughed. "It's
called a lobster!"

Little Otter was about to dip under the water for another look when Daddy Otter took his paw firmly. "There are lots of amazing things to see, but it's important you learn to look after yourself first." He held out a little shell. "Do you know what this is?"

"It's a clam!"

"Yes, that's right. We can eat it, but we can't open it with our paws. We need to find a stone to crack it with."

Little Otter floated in the water, trying to concentrate. If only they could swim a bit faster . . . there'd be plenty of time to learn about clams later!

"Let's see if we can spot a good stone on the seabed," said Daddy Otter, ducking beneath the waves.

Little Otter was about to plunge under too, when he noticed huge grey shapes diving gracefully nearby.

"Dolphins!" Little Otter cried. "Quick, Dad, let's go and see them!"

Little Otter didn't turn round to check Daddy Otter had heard. He sped off as fast as he could go towards the dolphins. The littlest dolphin spotted him and hung back from her pod, waiting for Little Otter to catch up.

"You're out pretty far for an otter!" she said.

Little Otter puffed up his fur. "I'm the best swimmer in the ocean!" he announced boldly.

The young dolphin laughed. "Is that right?" she asked, swimming off.

Faster and faster she swam as Little Otter chased behind. He paddled as hard as he could, but soon his legs ached and his heart was pounding.

He couldn't keep up! He watched as the dolphins disappeared over the waves.

Alone, Little Otter gazed around him, trying to catch his breath. The water was rough here, tossing him to and fro. Thunder rumbled in the sky above, and a cold raindrop landed on Little Otter's nose.

Where was Daddy Otter?

"Dad?" Little Otter called out as loudly as he could. But the only sound was the splashing of the waves. Little Otter lay on his back, wondering what to do. He wished he hadn't swum off alone!

"Well," thought Little Otter, trying to be brave, "I can't just float here in the rain all day." He kicked out his back legs and propelled with his tail, remembering what Daddy Otter had told him. He hoped he was going the right way!

Suddenly, a wave lifted Little Otter up, carrying him higher and higher. For a moment, he could see right across the ocean.

As he looked, he saw a blur streaking toward him! Was it another dolphin? No . . . It was Daddy Otter!

Little Otter splashed towards him and the two tumbled together, holding each other tightly.

"Thank goodness you're safe," said Daddy Otter, "I was so worried!"

"I'm sorry for swimming off," said Little Otter, as Daddy Otter took his paw. "I suppose I'm not the best swimmer in the ocean. But I know who the fastest is . . ."

"Who?" asked Daddy Otter.

"You!"

Daddy Otter laughed. "Come on, let's get back to the cove - you've had a big enough adventure for one day."

They paddled over the waves towards home – Little Otter's legs didn't feel so tired any more with his dad swimming beside him. Little Otter couldn't wait to tell his friends about the seagull and the lobster and the dolphins! But he was even more excited to tell them about Daddy Otter, the fastest swimmer in the ocean.

Tale Of A Tail

Written by Libby Walden

Illustrated by Maurizia Rubino

Tale Of A Tail

As the sun started to rise over the farmyard, one little piglet was already washed and fed, eager for the day to begin. Curly hopped over the other piglets on his way out of the pigpen.

"Where are you off to so early, Curly?" his brother Squiggle asked.

"I can't sleep," Curly replied. "I've been up all night thinking!"

"What is it this time?" yawned his sister, Twist. Everyone knew that Curly was a very curious piglet with a very curious mind, and he needed to learn something new every day.

"Today I need to know . . ." he announced, "what tails are for!" And with that, Curly turned on his trotters and bounded out of the pen in search of an answer.

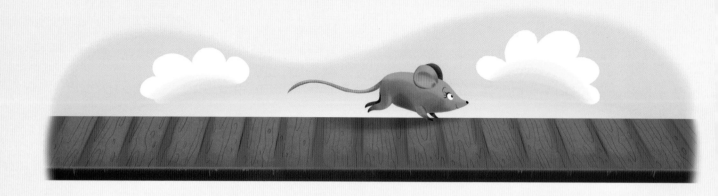

Curly hadn't gone far at all when he spotted a mouse with a long, pink tail scampering along the barn roof.

"Morning, Tilly!" Curly called. "I was wondering if you could tell me what my tail is for?"

"Of course!" replied Tilly, scuttling down to perch on the fence. "Tails are there to help you balance, Curly. I use mine when I'm running along the roof beams in the barn. Maybe you could use yours for balance too?"

So Curly carefully climbed up onto the lowest wall. As soon as all four of his trotters were on the wall, he wibbled and he wobbled and he wagged his little tail but . . .
SPLAT!

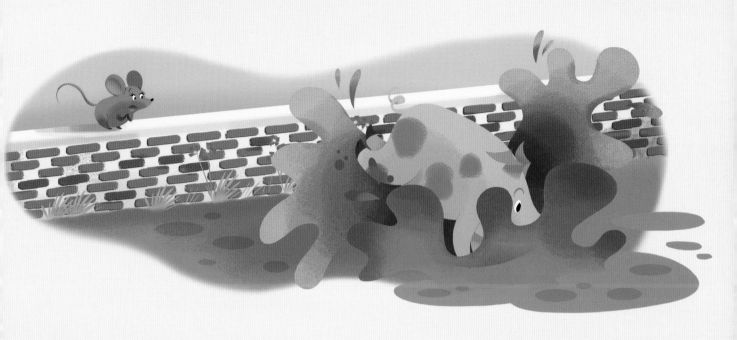

He fell head first into a muddy puddle!

"Perhaps your tail isn't for balancing with after all?" said Tilly kindly, as Curly wiped the mud off his face.

"No," he replied, "I don't think it is! Thank you anyway, Tilly." And off Curly trotted, to see if anyone else could help him find an answer.

All of a sudden, a black and white blur ran across Curly's path! "Curly! Curly! Come and play with me! It's so much fun, we can play fetch or catch or—"

"Calm down, Dash! I can't play right now, I'm trying to find out what tails do."

"Tails don't do anything, Curly, they are for chasing!" cried Dash, and he started to spin on the spot, barking and laughing as he chased his fluffy tail.

Curly thought this looked like a fun game, so he began to follow his own little curly tail, turning faster and faster in circles until . . . BUMP! He toppled right over!

"Oh dear! I don't think my tail is meant to be chased," said Curly, feeling very dizzy!

"Oh OK," replied Dash, still bounding around happily, "but maybe we could play fetch or catch or—"

"Sorry, Dash, maybe another time. I'm off to the stables to see if Major knows anything about my tail," said Curly, and away he trotted.

In the calm of the stables Major, the old Shire horse, was standing quietly chewing his oats.

"Excuse me, Major, sorry to bother you, but could you help me? I'm trying to find out what tails are for, and no one seems to have the right answer for my tail."

The horse lowered his head and peered down at the little pig. "I swish mine back and forth to keep the flies away, young piglet. Perhaps you should see if yours would do the same?"

Curly thought that sounded very useful, and so he focused really hard and wiggled and jiggled his bottom when all of a sudden . . . BZZZZZ! Just at that moment a fly landed on the end of the pig's little snout!

"Well, my tail definitely doesn't keep the flies away – they don't even notice when I swish it!
It must be too small!"
he said, shaking
his snout until
the fly flew off!

Poor Curly. He was beginning to think he would never find out what his tail was for. He said goodbye to Major and slowly made his way back to the pigpen, feeling very disappointed.

"Did you find out what tails are for, Curly?" asked Squiggle as Curly entered the pen.

"Well, I know that mice use theirs for balance, puppies chase theirs for fun and horses use theirs to swat away flies, but I'm still not really sure what ours do . . ." replied Curly sadly.

"Never mind, Curly," said Twist, in a kind voice. "It sounds like you learnt a lot, and you can always try again tomorrow!"

Just then Mum called them over for lunch, and all the piglets ran to the trough, excitedly. Curly slowly wandered over to the trough, thinking about what Twist had said as he began to chew his yummy vegetables. She was right! He had already found out a lot about tails, and he could go again tomorrow to ask more of his farmyard friends for answers. Chomping on the rind of a juicy apple, Curly began to feel much better. And all of a sudden, his tail began to . . . Wag!

"Curly!" cried his brothers and sisters together. "Look at your tail! It's wagging!" And it really was!

"I've found the answer!" Curly cried excitedly, looking back at his beautiful swirly little tail swishing back and forth. "Who knew we pigs could wag our tails when we're happy?" And Curly's tail wagged all the harder as he beamed back at the other piglets.

"Now, I wonder what I should learn about tomorrow . . ."

The Bear Who Wouldn't Share

Written by Lara Jennings

Illustrated by Zoe Waring

The Bear Who Wouldn't Share

Blake was a little bear who had one big problem. Sharing. One Sunday, he was out in the woods playing on his scooter. It had a lime-green frame and super-fast wheels.

Screech! Blake stopped at the old oak tree where his little sister, Bella, was waiting.

Bella looked longingly at the scooter. "Please can I have a go?" she asked.

But Blake just wouldn't share. "No! It's mine," he said.

Bella reached out and put her paws on the handlebars. "Pleeease?" she said. Blake pulled the scooter off his sister. But he jerked a bit too hard – and she fell backwards, right onto her bottom!

"Ouch!" said Bella, and her little brown nose went 'sniffle, sniffle' as she started to cry.

Blake looked at his sobbing sister and felt a tiny bit mean. Worse, he knew he had to take her home where he would get told off. And even worse, now he had to stop playing on his scooter.

The next morning, Blake was woken up early by Daddy Bear. "Wakey wakey, Blake! You're going to Milo's house today, remember? So go and wash your face and paws – we're leaving soon."

Milo the mole was Blake's best friend. And he just loved to visit Milo in his molehill, with its maze of dark, echoey tunnels.

When Blake arrived at Milo's the two friends played their favourite game – hide-and-seek. After they'd been playing for a while, they heard

Mummy Mole calling from the next tunnel, "Boys? Come into the kitchen! I've got a surprise for you."

Yum! Mummy Mole had baked them some cookies – lovely gooey cookies with chocolate chips.

Blake's mouth started to water. His tummy rumbled! And as soon as Mummy Mole's back was turned, he dived straight in and gobbled up all the cookies before his friend could get his paws on them! Scoff, scoff, scoff!

"Hey!" said Milo. "I'd like one too."

Mummy Mole saw what had happened and said, "Oh dear, Blake. Those cookies were for both of you to share."

Blake looked at his friend and felt a tiny bit mean. Worse, Milo didn't want to play with him any more. And even worse, Blake's tummy started to hurt, so Mummy Mole asked Daddy Bear to come and pick him up early. Blake went home feeling really quite sorry for himself.

The next morning, Blake was still feeling sad about his fall-out with Milo. He decided to cheer himself up by playing in the park with his kite.

"Ooh! That looks like fun!" said a voice. It was Blake's friend, Owen the owl, who was perched in a nearby apple tree.

"Can I play with your kite too? Please?" he asked.

"No!" said Blake. "I'm playing with it."

"Won't you share it with me?" said Owen. "We could play with it together. It'd be so much fun!"

Blake paused. He thought perhaps he should share with his friend – but he wanted to fly the kite himself! "No!" Blake said again, and he raced off.

135

Blake ran across the park, holding his brightly coloured kite out behind him, trying to get it to fly. But no matter how fast he sprinted, the kite dragged along the grass. Then the wind started to blow harder against Blake's fur. So he started to run again, holding the kite up until . . . Whooosh! The kite soared up in to the air.

"Look! Look! It's flying!" Blake called to Owen. But his friend had already flown back home.

The kite flew so fast that Blake couldn't control it. Whooosh, whooosh, whooosh! It looped madly in the air . . . and then flew straight into the apple tree! Blake looked at the kite and he felt awful.

He felt bad that he hadn't shared it with Owen. Worse, he'd upset his friend so much that he'd gone home. And even worse, his kite was now stuck – and he couldn't get it down without Owen's help. Blake plodded slowly and sadly home without his kite.

The next day, Blake went back to the park. He took his new bat and ball set which his mummy and daddy had bought him. He was ever so excited about showing it off to his friends. Blake spotted Milo, Owen and Bella playing by the lily pond. "Look at my new bat and ball set! Let's all play with it!" he called, running over.

Everyone turned to face him. They were all quiet until Owen said, "No, we're sorry, Blake. You wouldn't share with us before. So we don't want to play with you now."

Suddenly Blake realised that Owen was right. He'd upset his best friends and they might never forgive him!

"I'm sorry I wouldn't share with you. I really am," said Blake in a quiet voice. "But I'll start sharing from now on, I promise. Please can we all play together?"

Because they were kind, Milo, Owen and Bella decided to forgive Blake. They all played together with Blake's new toy, and had a lovely time hitting, running and catching.

After they had been playing for a while, Blake began to feel a little hungry. So he took out a chocolate bar he'd brought with him – a lovely chocolate bar with chunks of cookie inside. "Yum!" thought Blake as his tummy started to rumble. But as he lifted the chocolate bar to his mouth, he remembered what he had promised about sharing. Blake really wanted the chocolate bar all to himself – it was his favourite, and not really big enough for four people.

But a promise was a promise, and so he broke his chocolate bar into four equal pieces: one for Bella, one for Owen, one for Milo and one for himself.

"Thanks, Blake!" said Milo, and offered around slices of his apple.

"Look what my daddy baked!" said Owen, rushing off to his rucksack and pulling out some cherry cake. Before long, they had a whole picnic made up of everyone's snacks! Blake munched away until he was full, and then lay down happily on the grass. He thought he rather liked sharing after all!

Favourite Animal Stories
An Illustrated Treasury

LITTLE TIGER PRESS LTD
an imprint of the Little Tiger Group
1 Coda Studios, 189 Munster Road,
London SW6 6AW
www.littletiger.co.uk

Published in Great Britain 2017
This volume copyright © Little Tiger Press 2016
Cover illustration by Lucy Fleming
Text and illustrations copyright © Little Tiger Press 2016

All rights reserved
Printed in China
ISBN 978-1-84869-357-9
LTP/2700/1965/0917
2 4 6 8 10 9 7 5 3